Published by C. Cleary Books, Brock Media LLC

For information and permission write to:
Brock Media LLC
PO Box 4564, Hallandale Beach, FL 33008 (954)951-3070

ISBN 978-0-9889446-1-9

Printed in the United States of America

Book Designer
Brock Media LLC

C. Clearly Books Publishing

www.cclearlybooks.com

My YEARBOOK

Remembering Classmates & Teachers

**Memories from
School Year**

**-
_____ _____**

THIS BOOK BELONGS TO: _____

SCHOOL NAME: _____ GRADE: _____

My SCHOOL PHOTO

Add a Picture

YEAR IN REVIEW
MY FAVORITE...

TEACHER: _____

TEACHER: _____

SUBJECT: _____

SONG: _____

MUSICIAN: _____

SNEAKER: _____

PHONE APP: _____

PHONE CASE: _____

GAME APP: _____

COLOR: _____

MOVIE/TV SHOW: _____

ACTOR: _____

YEAR IN REVIEW

MY CLASSMATES...

BEST FRIEND (BFF): _____

THE BEST DANCER: _____

THE COOLEST: _____

THE CLASS CLOWN: _____

THE FUNNIEST: _____

THE SMARTEST: _____

THE PEACEMAKER: _____

THE ENTREPRENEUR: _____

THE LYRICIST: _____

THE ARTIST: _____

THE BOOKWORM: _____

THE BEST DRESSED: _____

THE MOST ATHLETIC: _____

THE MOST GIVING: _____

THE MOST HELPFUL: _____

THE MOST POPULAR: _____

THE BIGGEST EGO: _____

WHO IS MOSTLY LIKELY TO BE...

FUTURE PRESIDENT: _____

FUTURE MAYOR: _____

FUTURE CEO: _____

FUTURE DOCTOR: _____

FUTURE NURSE: _____

FUTURE LAWYER: _____

FUTURE POLICE/FIRE: _____

FUTURE POLITICIAN: _____

FUTURE AUTHOR: _____

FUTURE MUSICIAN: _____

FUTURE ATHELETE: _____

TEACHERS AND PRINCIPALS

PRINCIPAL   _____

ASST. PRINCIPAL   _____

GUIDANCE   _____

MATH   _____

SCIENCE   _____

SOCIAL STUDIES   _____

LANGUAGE ARTS   _____

READING   _____

PHYSICAL ED (PE)   _____

COACH   _____

COACH   _____

FOREIGN LANGUAGE   _____

COMPUTER   _____

PEER COUNSELING   _____

DANCE   _____

BAND   _____

ART   _____

HEALTH   _____

BUSINESS ED   _____

DRAMA   _____

CHORUS   _____

OTHER _____   _____

OTHER _____   _____

AUTOGRAPHS FROM MY
TEACHERS AND PRINCIPALS

The moment

*"Either write something worth reading
or do something worth writing."*
-Benjamin Franklin

I WILL ALWAYS REMEMBER...

AUTOGRAPHS

AUTOGRAPHS

AUTOGRAPHS

AUTOGRAPHS

AUTOGRAPHS

AUTOGRAPHS

AUTOGRAPHS

AUTOGRAPHS

AUTOGRAPHS

AUTOGRAPHS

AUTOGRAPHS

AUTOGRAPHS

AUTOGRAPHS

AUTOGRAPHS

AUTOGRAPHS

AUTOGRAPHS

AUTOGRAPHS

AUTOGRAPHS

AUTOGRAPHS

AUTOGRAPHS

Looking ahead...

THE HARDEST THING ABOUT NEXT YEAR WILL BE...

_____

_____

_____

_____

_____

_____

_____

_____

_____

_____

_____

_____

_____

_____

I'M EXCITED ABOUT NEXT YEAR BECAUSE...

_____

_____

_____

_____

_____

_____

I CAN'T WAIT TO...

_____

_____

_____

_____

_____

_____

_____

A MESSAGE FROM THE AUTHOR

Dear Students,

Congratulations! This school year is finally ending. It is important to take each experience this year an
use it to help you become a better person. If this year was not your best, there is always today an
tomorrow to make a difference. You are the author of your own story, so do not let anyone else wri
it. To make your today and tomorrow great, here are some simple rules to live by:

1. Take advantage of your education
2. Never listen to any negative opinions of you
3. Think positively about your talents, goals, and dreams
4. Have a goal to focus on at all times
5. Avoid using excuses

Remember, a winner cannot win without making it to the finish line. Whether you get there first or yo
get there last—you just have to get there. Winning is not everything, but it is important. To be great
anything you will work hard, no exceptions.

Finally, as you leave all of your teachers and some friends behind this year, from time to time come ba
to this book and reflect on the positive memories you shared together.

A good quote to live by, *"How you do anything is how you do everything."*

Best Wishes!